D0386762

THE KANE CHRONICLES

SURVIVAL GUIDE

Based on the books of the Kane Chronicles series by Rick Riordan
Published by Disney • Hyperion Books

The Kane Chronicles Survival Guide

Created by Threefold Limited, London, England
Written by Mary-Jane Knight
Designed by Philip Chidlow
Illustrations on pages 14, 15, 16, 19, 22, 25, 39, 40, 43, 45, 46, 48, 77, 78, 81, 107, 130 by Antonio Caparo
Additional illustrations by Artful Doodlers, London, Philip Chidlow

Printed in Malaysia
First Edition
10 9 8 7 6 5 4 3 2 1
H106-9333-5-12032

Library of Congress Cataloging-in-Publication Data

The Kane Chronicles survival guide/ character snapshot illustrations by Antonio Caparo; written by Mary-Jane Knight; designed by Philip Chidlow; additional illustration by Artful Doodlers, Philip Chidlow.—1st ed.
p. cm.
ISBN 978-1-4231-5362-7 (hardcover)
1. Riordan, Rick. Kane chronicles. I. Knight, M. J. (Mary-Jane) II. Caparo, Antonio Javier, ill.
PS3568.I5866Z74 2011
813'.54—dc23 2011027111

Visit www.disneyhyperionbooks.com

THE KANE CHRONICLES SURVIVAL GUIDE

DISNEY • HYPERION BOOKS
NEW YORK

CONTENTS

THE KANE CHRONICLES

THE STORY SO FAR

Here comes trouble. . . .

Carter Kane's mother died six years ago, and since then he has traveled the world with his Egyptologist father, Julius Kane. Meanwhile, Carter's younger sister, Sadie, has been living with her grandparents in London.

Carter and Sadie meet again one Christmas Eve, when their father takes them to the British Museum in London. Here he uses his influence to gain access to the valuable Rosetta Stone. He then performs a bizarre ritual that conjures shadowy figures and causes a massive explosion, destroying the stone. Julius disappears, leaving Carter and Sadie to discover that he has somehow awakened the gods of Ancient Egypt, at least one of whom has evil intentions toward them, and, it seems, toward the rest of the world. . . .

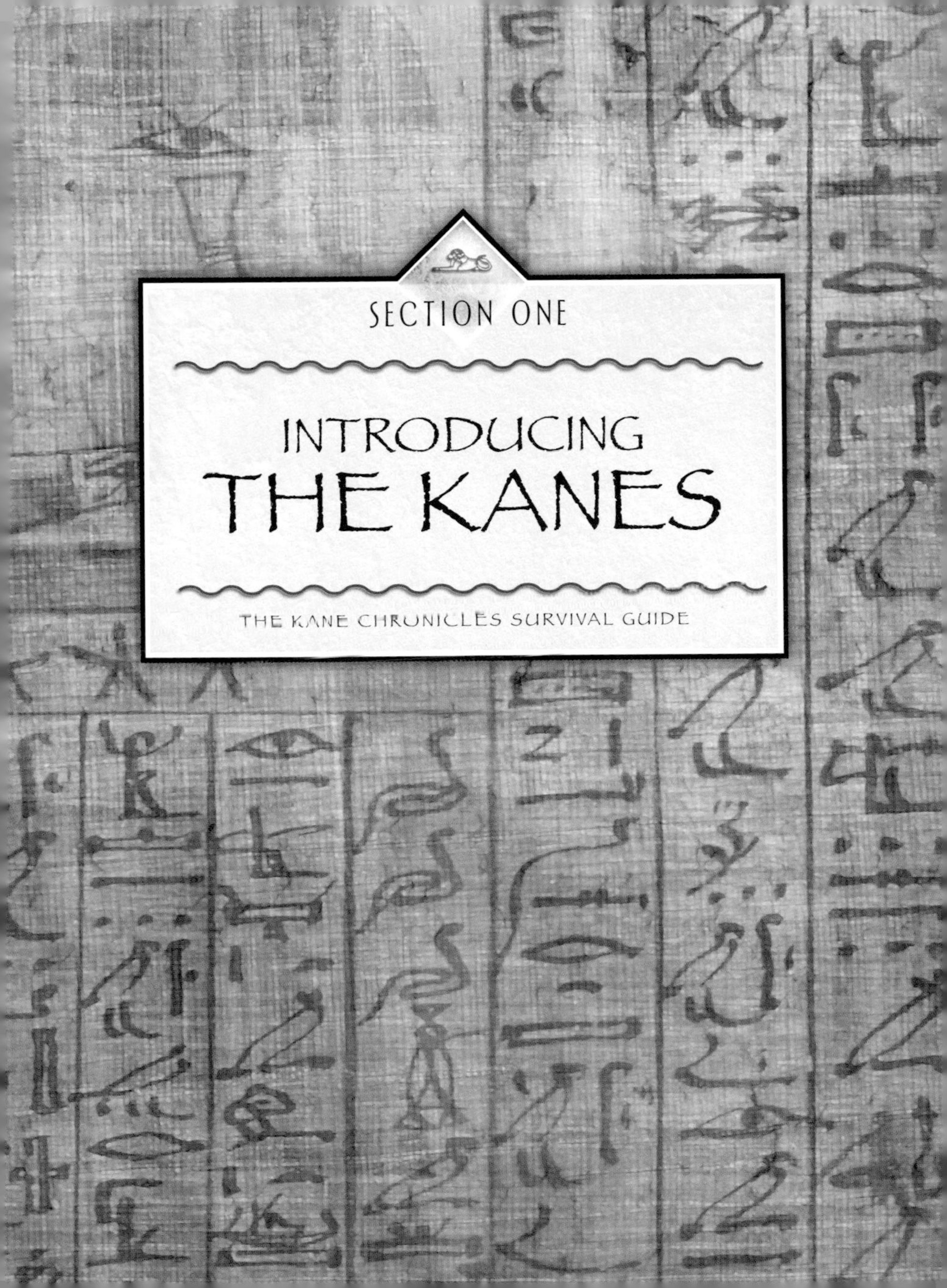

SECTION ONE

INTRODUCING THE KANES

Carter and Sadie Kane

"When you see each other twice a year, it's like you're distant cousins rather than siblings. We had absolutely nothing in common except our parents."—Carter Kane

The Kane children are not very similar, and don't even know each other all that well, which is bound to happen when two people lead completely different lives. It wasn't always that way, though: they lived together with their parents in Los Angeles, but were separated at a young age after their mother died, and now only see each other twice a year.

Being raised apart has accentuated their differences: Carter has lived out of suitcases, never staying long in any country, while Sadie

has lived with her grandparents in the same comfortable London home since she was six. She goes to school with lots of friends, and even has a British accent.

Carter sounds all-American, and being homeschooled and always on the go hasn't given him the chance to make many friends. On top of all that, the siblings don't look very much alike, as Carter takes after their dad and Sadie looks very much like their mom.

When Carter and Sadie do see each other, they usually argue, each envying aspects of the other's life. But both Carter and Sadie get annoyed when people question whether they are members of the same family—after all, Kanes have to stick together.

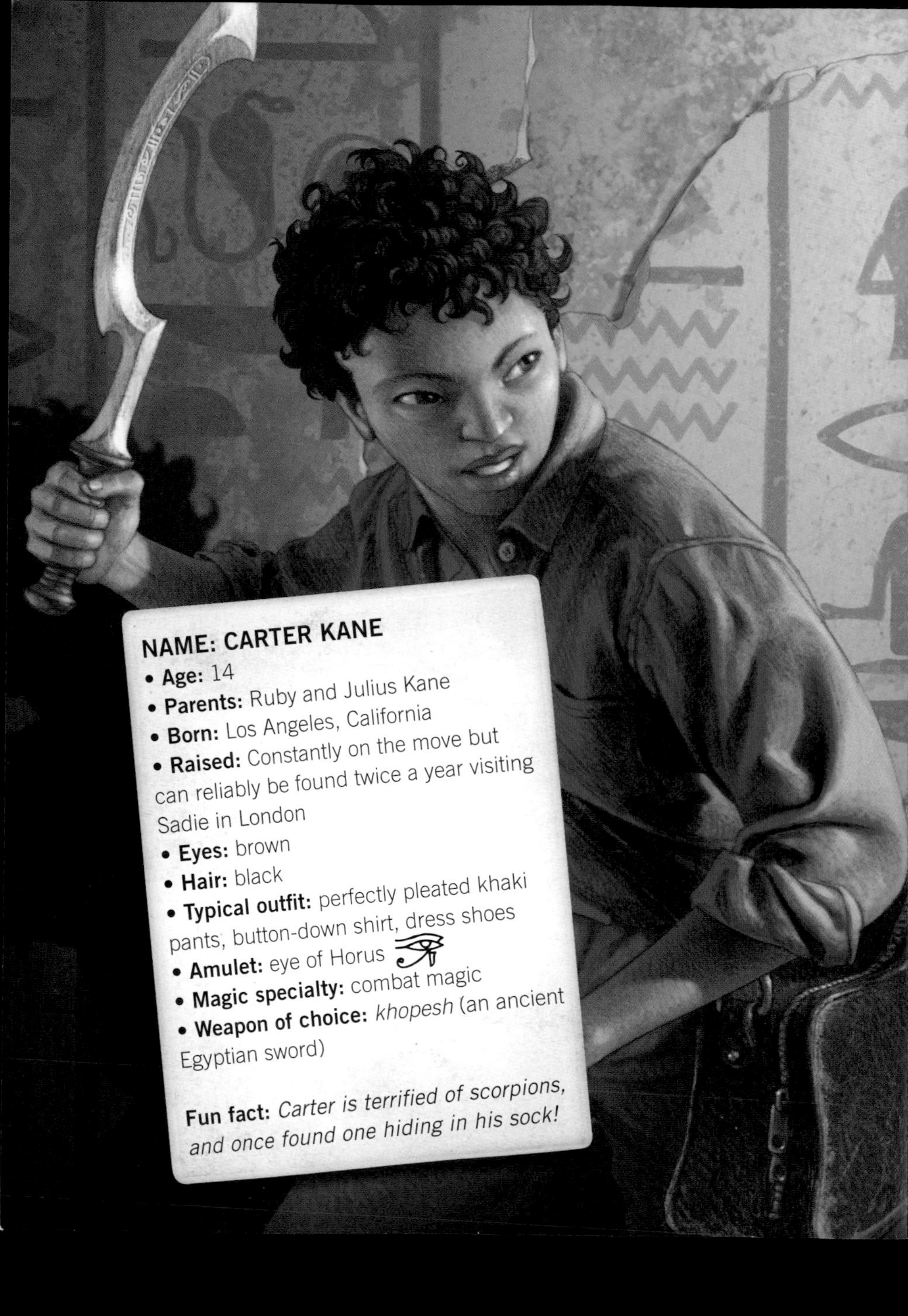
NAME: CARTER KANE
• Age: 14
• Parents: Ruby and Julius Kane
• Born: Los Angeles, California
• Raised: Constantly on the move but can reliably be found twice a year visiting Sadie in London
• Eyes: brown
• Hair: black
• Typical outfit: perfectly pleated khaki pants, button-down shirt, dress shoes
• Amulet: eye of Horus
• Magic specialty: combat magic
• Weapon of choice: khopesh (an ancient Egyptian sword)
Fun fact: Carter is terrified of scorpions, and once found one hiding in his sock!

NAME: SADIE KANE
• Age: 12
• Parents: Ruby and Julius Kane
• Born: Los Angeles, California
• Raised: London, England
• Eyes: blue
• Hair: caramel, often dyed with streaks of bright colors
• Typical outfit: battered jeans, leather jacket, combat boots
• Amulet: tyet (a.k.a. knot of Isis)
• Magic specialty: a natural magician, reads hieroglyphs, understands Egyptian
• Weapon of choice: wand or staff
Fun fact: Sadie keeps loads of chewing gum on hand (it helps her concentrate).

The Faust and Kane families both carry the blood of the pharaohs and have been members of the House of Life (see page 74) for centuries. Ruby Faust met Julius Kane at an archeological site in The Valley of the Kings. They fell in love and got married, thereby uniting two strong magical families and making Carter and Sadie the most powerful children to have been born in centuries.

RUBY KANE

Ruby Kane was an anthropologist who taught at a university and had a deep interest in Egyptology. She was also a talented magician who possessed the rare power of divination, which allowed her to foresee future events. Her amulet was an *ankh*, the Egyptian symbol for life. Ruby died under mysterious circumstances at Cleopatra's Needle in London when Sadie was six and Carter was eight.

JULIUS KANE

Julius Kane is a world-renowned Egyptologist who specializes in translating ancient Egyptian texts. He has written many books on the subject and is called to act as an expert at many museums and on archeological digs, allowing him to travel all over the world.

Wherever he goes, Julius keeps his leather workbag by his side. When Carter and Sadie open the bag (despite, of course, being told not to) they find a decorated wooden box containing a lump of white wax, a wooden stylus, a palette, and glass jars of colored ink. There are also lengths of brown twine, an ebony cat statue, and a thick roll of papyrus. Finally, there's a wax figurine *shabti*, which means "answerer."

Julius uses his job as a cover for his life as a magician. His travels help him stay on the run from the House of Life's magicians, who have been tracking him since Julius broke one of their laws in the battle that led to Ruby's death. As further punishment, they have kept Julius away from his brother, Amos.

AMOS KANE

Amos is Julius's brother, and uncle to Carter and Sadie. Impeccably groomed, he almost always wears a sharp suit, a fedora hat, and elegantly braided hair with gems woven throughout. He's also often within reach of his tenor sax, and reminds Carter of the sort of jazz musician his dad would drag him to hear when he was younger. His symbol is the *was*, or "power," scepter.

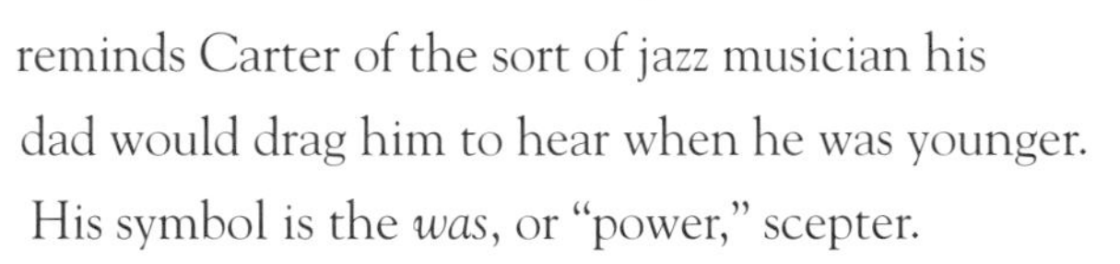

Amos has long kept his distance from Carter and Sadie, though not by choice. But things change when Julius disappears. Amos takes the children to his Brooklyn headquarters to keep them safe, despite the objections of Sadie's grandparents.

Amos is the one who has to explain to the children the truth about their heritage and the dangers that they will face as Kanes.

GRAN AND GRAMPS FAUST

Gran and Gramps Faust, Ruby's parents, live in a London flat on the east side of the River Thames, near Canary Wharf. Gran is frail-looking and colorless, rather like a stick person. She's always offering people cups of tea and horrid-tasting, burned cookies, which she makes herself.

Gramps is a former rugby player with strong, beefy arms, a large belly, and eyes sunk deep into his face. He can be scary at times and isn't at all friendly toward Amos or Julius Kane, who he holds responsible for Ruby's death. The Fausts know that magic exists, but they don't seem to be practicing magicians.

MUFFIN

Muffin was Sadie's going-away present from her dad when she moved in with Gran and Gramps Faust. Muffin keeps Sadie company and often exhibits typical cat behavior, but something about her is a little off: she never seems to get older or bigger, her pointy ears are too tall for her head, and with her yellow and black fur, she looks an awful lot like a miniature leopard. Also, unlike most other cats, Muffin's eyes are always exceptionally alert, and a mysterious silver Egyptian pendant dangles from her collar.

Once Carter and Sadie's adventures begin, Muffin transforms into something much more useful than a house cat (see Bast, pages 46–47).

"She didn't look anything like a muffin, but Sadie had been little when she named her, so I guess you have to cut her some slack."

—Carter

TeenQueen Asks . . .

Our Q&A interview this month is with

SADIE KANE: QUEEN OF MAGIC

An exclusive TeenQueen interview with the young magician everyone's talking about . . .

Q: ***WHAT WOULD YOU SAY IS YOUR PERSONAL STYLE?***

A: Definitely not boring, I'll tell you that. I keep an eye out for vintage bargains, but my everyday look generally includes perfectly broken-in jeans, a T-shirt, and a leather jacket, worn with combat boots. I never go anywhere without my music, so earphones are probably my most important accessory—and they're great for drowning out adults and teachers.

Q: *WHO ARE YOUR BEST MATES?*

A: Liz and Emma. But I don't get to see them as much, now that I'm running all over the world. I miss them loads, but with all the new trainee magicians around, I'm making new friends: Walt, Jaz, and the younger kids, too. They almost seem like family these days. . . . Oh, and Carter, I guess. When he's being cool.

Q: *HOW WOULD YOUR FRIENDS DESCRIBE YOU?*

A: As perfect, of course! Well, I suppose that they might say I can be a tad sarcastic and stubborn (I prefer "persistent"), but that I'm also caring, funny, kind, and loyal.

Q: *HOW DO YOU SPEND YOUR DOWNTIME?*

A: Well, what with trying to stop the apocalypse and all, I don't exactly have a lot of time to relax. But when I do, I like to skateboard and Rollerblade with Liz and Emma, or lounge around watching soaps and movies. In New York, I like to shoot baskets with my baboon buddy, Khufu. Basketball is way cooler than the netball we play at school in London, and Khufu is teaching me some moves. It's great.

When I go out I visit the Met and Central Park—it's peaceful there (as long as you're not being attacked by vengeful gods).

Q: ***WHERE ARE YOUR THREE FAVE PLACES?***

A: 1. Cleopatra's Needle by the River Thames. When I want to feel close to my mom, that's where I go. There are sphinxes guarding it, so it feels like a little piece of Egypt.

2. The London Eye, for an amazing bird's-eye view over London.

3. The nearest city farm is a good place to go to get away (Liz volunteers there, so Emma and I go some afternoons when she's working).

Q: ***WHAT FIVE THINGS CAN'T YOU LIVE WITHOUT?***

A: I've been traveling pretty light these days, but if I had a one-way ticket to a desert island, I guess I would bring:

1. Gum, and chocolate caramels—a lifetime's supply.
2. A picture of my mom
3. My magical kit, because you never know what else is lurking on that island.
4. Doughboy (hey, shabtis come in handy)
5. My friends and family. Which might be cheating, but life would be boring without them.

Q: *WHAT ARE YOUR PET PEEVES?*

A:

- Security guards—they hate skaters and exist only to stop us having fun.
- My brother (sometimes)
- Homework (always)
- Being told what to do. Seriously, don't even try.

Q: *DO YOU HAVE A SECRET (OR NOT SO SECRET) CRUSH?*

A: Well, I probably shouldn't be saying this, but: Anubis. Or possibly Walt. No, wait—both. ☺

Q: *DO YOU HAVE A SPECIAL SKILL?*

A: I read hieroglyphs like a native Egyptian, and could open portals even before I started training. Which has definitely come in handy recently.

Q: *WHAT IS YOUR AMBITION IN LIFE?*

A: To travel farther than I have so far, and never to know what is going to happen next. But for now, I'll settle for beating back the forces of evil.

SECTION TWO

GODS & GODDESSES

THE KANE CHRONICLES SURVIVAL GUIDE

ONE: THE CREATION OF EGYPT

In the beginning there was nothing but a huge expanse of water called Nun. Out of these waters of chaos rose the sun god.

Ra was all-powerful and took many forms, but he was alone and surrounded by chaos. He wanted to bring order to the world and could bring things into being simply by naming them. First he created day and night, saying: "I am Khepera at dawn, Ra at noon, and Atum in the evening." So the sun rose, passed through the sky, and set for the first time.

Because he was alone in the world, Ra created gods to control other elements: he coughed and breathed out Shu, who made the first winds blow, and spat out Tefnut, who willed the first rains to fall. In turn, Shu and Tefnut had two children: Nut, the sky goddess, and Geb, the earth god.

After this, Ra created other gods, and together they created every living thing on earth. Last of all, Ra named mankind, and there were men and women in the land of Egypt.

TWO: THE STORY OF RA AND SEKHMET

Ra took the form of a man and became the first pharaoh, ruling Egypt for thousands of years. Eventually he grew old, and men no longer feared him or obeyed his laws.

Ra was angry and called together the gods and goddesses—Shu and Tefnut and Geb and Nut. Ra asked them what he should do about the men and women and their evil deeds. The gods agreed that Ra should create a daughter who would destroy the men.

So Ra's daughter Sekhmet came into being, the fiercest of goddesses. She rushed upon her prey like a lion, and killed those who had disobeyed Ra. When Ra saw what Sekhmet had done, he took pity on the men, but he could not stop Sekhmet.

▲ Brewing in Ancient Egypt

He sent messengers to the Nile to bring him red ocher. They brought the ocher to Heliopolis, where Ra commanded the women to brew seven thousand jars of drink. Ra mingled red ocher with the liquid and poured it over the fields. At daybreak Sekhmet came and found the place flooded. She saw the red brew and thought it was the blood of those she had killed. She stooped and drank until she was drunk and unable to kill anyone. Then she came reeling back to where Ra waited, without killing a single man.

Then Ra changed Sekhmet's name to Hathor, and changed her nature so she was sweet and loving. Mankind was saved, and Hathor's priestesses drank the beer of Heliopolis colored with red ocher in her honor when they celebrated her festival at the start of every new year.

THREE: RA'S SECRET NAME

Ra was old and he needed to leave the earth and let the younger gods rule in his place. No one could take power from him, as his power was in his secret name, which only he knew.

Geb and Nut had children: their names were Osiris and Isis, Nephthys and Set. Isis was the wisest: she was cleverer than a million men. She knew all things in heaven and earth, except the secret name of Ra, and she decided to find it out. As Ra passed over Egypt, he dribbled like a very old man. When his spittle fell upon the ground, it made mud, and Isis took this and kneaded it like dough. Then she formed it into a serpent, making the first cobra—the *uraeus*, which became the symbol of royalty worn by pharaohs.

Isis placed the cobra in the dust where Ra passed every day. As he passed, the cobra bit him, and then vanished into the grass. The cobra's poison ran through Ra's body, and he gave a cry of pain, but he could not speak, though he trembled and shuddered. He cried to the gods for help.

They came, and with them came Isis, the healer. "*Tell me your secret name, divine father,*" said Isis. "*For only by speaking your name in my spells can I cure you.*"

Ra spoke the many names that were his: "*I am maker of heaven and earth. I am builder of the mountains. I am the source of the waters through all the world. I am light and darkness. I am creator of the great river of Egypt. I am the kindler of the fire that burns in the sky; yes, I am Khepera in the morning, Ra at noon, and Atum in the evening.*"

But Isis knew that he had told her only the names everyone knew, and that his secret name lay hidden in his heart. She said: "*You know the name I need is not among those you have spoken. Tell me the secret name, and the poison will come forth, and you will have no more pain.*"

Ra made Isis swear that she would tell the name to no one but the son she would have, who should also swear not to pass it on. And Isis swore she would keep the secret. Then the knowledge of the name of power passed from Ra's heart into hers.

Isis banished the poison from Ra's body, and he had peace, but he reigned over the earth no longer. He took his place in the heavens, traveling every day across the sky as the sun, and at night crossing the underworld and passing through the Duat. The Egyptians painted the scenes of that journey on the walls of the tombs of the pharaohs, with the knowledge that was written in *The Book of the Dead.* A copy was buried in every rich man's grave so they might read it and come safely to the land beyond the west where the dead live.

Family Tree of Egyptian Gods

"The Egyptians would not have been stupid enough to believe in imaginary gods. The beings they described in their myths are very, very real. In the old days, the priests of Egypt would call upon these gods to channel their power and perform great feats. That is the origin of what we now call magic. Like many things, magic was first invented by the Egyptians. Each temple had a branch of magicians called the House of Life. Their magicians were famed throughout the ancient world."

—Amos

Ancient Egyptian Gods

SHU: GOD OF WINDS AND AIR

How to recognize him: *Wears a huge ostrich feather headdress, carries flags, has windblown (sometimes knotty) hair, always looks exhausted*

Shu has two jobs: to keep the winds blowing, and to enforce Ra's punishment against Shu's own children—Nut, the sky goddess, and Geb, god of the earth—by keeping them apart. Egyptian lore tells us that if Shu allows Nut and Geb to meet again, the earth and sky would collide and bring chaos to the universe.

TEFNUT: GODDESS OF RAIN

How to recognize her: *Lion-headed lady, most likely dripping wet, usually found sitting on a throne*

Tefnut is mother and grandmother to many gods, but family isn't her only responsibility—without Tefnut to bring the rain, Egypt would have shriveled up and dried out under the hot sun.

NUT: GODDESS OF THE SKY

How to recognize her: *She arches over the earth, likes to stargaze and stare into the night sky*

Nut's arms and legs are the four pillars on which the sky rests. But Nut doesn't just have her head in the clouds all the time; at the end of each day, she swallows the sun god, Ra, and gives birth to him the next morning, giving us night and day.

GEB: GOD OF THE EARTH

How to recognize him: *Hangs out below Nut's arch, can take the form of a tower of sand that shifts to reveal his face*

Geb is a family man, with five powerful children and a wife he loves deeply and misses terribly once they are separated. He didn't lose his sense of humor, though: myth has it that his laughter causes earthquakes.

OSIRIS: GOD OF THE DEAD

How to recognize him: *Has a beard and wears a crown, likes to hold strange objects like crooks and flails*

In addition to being the god of the dead, Osiris is a god of fertility and resurrection. And Osiris knows a thing or two about resurrection: he was born as the oldest of Nut and Geb's five children, but then reborn as his once-sister Isis's husband and his once-brother Horus's father. He became king, but was murdered by his jealous brother, Set. But you can't keep Osiris down: he was revived as the Lord of the Dead.

◀ *Djed* amulet of Osiris

ISIS: GODDESS OF MOTHERHOOD AND LOVE

How to recognize her: *A beautiful woman wearing a* tyet *knot as a symbol of protection. She sits on a throne shaped like a cow's horn, often with Horus on her lap.*

Isis is the goddess of motherhood and love. She values the time she spends watching over her son, Horus, and helping her husband, Osiris, rule the land, but she is a strong goddess in her own right, who knows powerful magic spells and uses them to help people in need. Isis is a healer, but she can also be sneaky and manipulative in order to help those she loves, tricking enemies and rivals into giving up power and secrets: she poisoned Ra so that Osiris could become king in his place.

▲ *Tyet*

▲ Isis with Horus on her lap

HORUS: THE FALCON GOD

How to recognize him: *He has unique eyes and always dresses like a warrior. Sometimes wears a double crown and holds a winged disk. He likes to hang out with fowl creatures such as hawks and falcons.*

Horus is the falcon-headed god of the sky, the god of revenge, and the protector of the ruler of Egypt. Horus's connection to the living Pharaoh is so strong that each pharaoh becomes known as the human manifestation of Horus. His evil uncle Set envies Horus's power and tries to defeat him at every turn, keeping Horus on the run. When Set catches him, they battle, and Set damages one of Horus's eyes. It is replaced with an eye made of moonlight, creating the Eye of Horus.

SEKHMET: GODDESS OF WAR AND DESTRUCTION

How to recognize her: *Golden woman in glowing red armor with a bow and arrow or giant blazing lion.*

Sekhmet was created by Ra to attack men and women who were disobeying him and behaving badly (see The Stories of Ra, page 28).

SET: GOD OF CHAOS

How to recognize him: *May appear as a large, brutish man, a red-headed donkey, or even a pig. Whatever form he's in, he loves red, so keep an eye out for red clothing, hair, and even red eyes.*

Set never liked living by the rules, so it's no surprise that he's the god of chaos. He did an awful lot of awful things, like murdering his brother Osiris, and then trying to kill his nephew Horus so he could take Horus's place as the ruler of the living. Horus eventually won and avenged his father's death by ruling all of Egypt and exiling Set to the desert. But even banishment couldn't change Set's ways: he still gets angry and whips up awful storms, or performs an occasional evil deed.

NEPHTHYS: GODDESS OF THE NIGHT

How to recognize her: *Wears hieroglyphic nameplate jewelry, carries a kite (the bird), likes to hold bones and skulls*

Nephthys is best known as the goddess of the night and protective goddess of the dead, but she is also the goddess of nature, lamentation, and sleep. Even though she is married to

Set, she doesn't follow in his evil footsteps, and is a faithful sister and friend of Isis. After Set murdered Osiris, Nephthys helped Isis search for and collect Osiris's scattered limbs so that Isis could rebuild his body and bring him back to life.

ANUBIS: GOD OF FUNERALS AND DEATH

How to recognize him: *Has the head of a jackal. In full jackal form, he wears a golden collar and is black, sleek, and graceful. When he appears as a human, his ears stick up like a jackal's.*

Anubis is the son of Nephthys and Osiris. He helped to preserve Osiris's body after Set had killed him, and helped Osiris live again. This process created the first mummy and led to the practice of embalming, so it's no surprise that Anubis is also known as the god of embalming and mummification. On top of that, Anubis is also the god of the afterlife and spends most of his time living in the Land of the Dead. He can visit graveyards and places of death and mourning whenever he wants, but has to use a host body if he wants to go anywhere else. His main job is to weigh the hearts of the newly dead against the feather of truth to see if they are worthy of entering the afterlife. This scene and Anubis's likeness are often painted on tombs to protect the dead and help them to enter the underworld.

BAST: GODDESS OF CATS, WOMEN, AND CHILDREN

How to recognize her: *Cat woman with the attitude of a gentle lioness and the agility of a gymnast. Sometimes answers to "Muffin."*

Bast is a gentle protective goddess, but she sometimes appears with the head of a lioness to frighten enemies and protect the king in battle. She is a daughter of the sun god, Ra, and when she's shown as a lioness, she is connected with sunlight. But Bast has a dark side, too, and when she appears as a cat, she's associated with the moon. Likewise, Bast has two sides to her personality: gentleness and aggressiveness. She shows her gentle side as a welcome protector of hearth and homes and pregnant women. But watch out—when she is aggressive, she can be a vicious killer in battle. With her catlike reflexes, skill with weapons and spells, and ability to summon cats to help out in scrapes, she is a powerful ally.

BES: PROTECTOR OF CHILDREN

How to recognize him: *Short lion man with a big head and scruffy beard, often carries knives. He likes to play drums and bells, so keep an ear out.*

Bes protects pregnant women, newborn babies, and families. But just as he is the protector of all that is good, he struggles to keep away evil and is also god of war and can be a feisty fighter. Bes is also a patron of music and dance, and protects people from snake and scorpion bites. All in all, he is quite the busy god!

KHONSU: GOD OF THE MOON

How to recognize him: *Tall, thin, glamorous twenty-year-old with silver irises and a shaved head, except for a ponytail down one side*

Khonsu is a pretty mean senet player, and Nut played against him to win the five extra days on which she gave birth to her children. Because the moon constantly changes, waxing and waning, he has the power to lengthen or shorten lives—both mortal and godly.

THOTH: GOD OF WISDOM AND LEARNING

How to recognize him: *As a human, lean and lanky twenty-year-old in a lab coat with a luscious mane of blond hair. He talks a lot, using awfully big words.*

As the god of wisdom and learning, Thoth is quite the know-it-all and can't resist sharing facts and stories, without regard to whether or not you want to hear them or if you're in an enormous rush. The Ancient Egyptians believed he invented the art of writing and is the official scribe of the afterworld. He wrote *The Book of the Dead.*

THE STORY OF THE DEMON DAYS

Ra, the most powerful of all of the gods, heard a prophecy that a child of Nut and Geb would overthrow him. Not one to give up power, Ra forbade the pregnant Nut from having children on any of the 360 days and nights of the Ancient Egyptian year.

But Nut had long dreamed of being a mother, so she hatched a plan to outsmart Ra. She gambled with the moon god, Khonsu, but instead of playing for money, Khonsu had to give Nut a bit of moonlight every time he lost. She collected enough moonlight to create five new days at the end of the calendar year and gave birth to one child on each day.

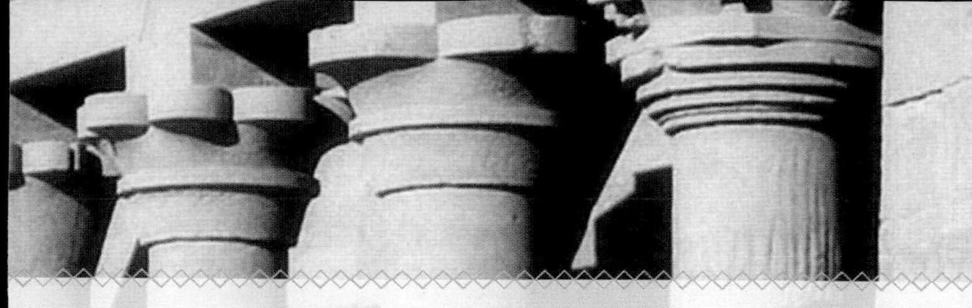

The children were:

OSIRIS, born December 27
HORUS THE ELDER, born December 28
SET, born December 29
ISIS, born December 30
NEPHTHYS, born December 31

Although the Demon Days are considered bad luck by mortals, who don't take risks or do anything dangerous in that time (like creating portals, which means that magicians have to find other ways to travel at the end of the year), Nut and Geb's children are at the height of their power on their birthdays. Constant plotters, they often attempt mighty and daring feats on those days, like trying to turn North America into a desert, as Set did on a recent birthday.

SECTION THREE
DARK DEITIES
& BEASTLY BEINGS
THE KANE CHRONICLES SURVIVAL GUIDE

APOPHIS

Apophis is Ra's greatest and most formidable enemy and the embodiment of all things evil and chaotic. He is usually depicted as a snake of unbelievable size and length, but is sometimes portrayed as an enormous Nile crocodile.

According to Ancient Egyptian legend, Apophis attacked Ra's boat every night as it passed through the Underworld. Most nights, Apophis was beaten back and killed, but he occasionally succeeded in harming Ra, which caused stormy weather. When he felt particularly strong and daring, Apophis would swallow Ra's boat whole, and Ra's temporary absence would cause a solar eclipse. This didn't happen often as Apophis was almost always defeated, but no matter how many times he died, Apophis always came back to life to try again.

The prayers of Egyptian priests were said to help keep Apophis at bay. Others would help the priests by making wax images of snakes that represented Apophis, and spitting on, burning, and destroying them. These efforts, combined with the recitation of spells from *The Book of Overcoming Apophis*, were meant to keep Apophis from succeeding in his efforts to overthrow Ra and bring chaos to earth.

The Book of Overcoming Apophis

This book contained spells of protection against Apophis, a list of his secret names, and even songs that celebrated Ra's victories against Apophis. The book has several chapters that describe the various ways to defeat Apophis, including:

THE CHAPTER OF SPITTING ON APOPHIS

THE CHAPTER OF DEFILING APOPHIS WITH THE LEFT FOOT

THE CHAPTER OF TAKING A LANCE TO SMITE APOPHIS

THE CHAPTER OF CHAINING APOPHIS

THE CHAPTER OF TAKING A KNIFE TO SMITE APOPHIS

THE CHAPTER OF SETTING FIRE TO APOPHIS

Destroying Apophis is quite a gruesome, complicated process: First he has to be speared, then cut through with searing-hot knives, and then all the bones in his body have to be separated from each other. Then, his head, legs, and tail have to be cut off. The remaining pieces of his body have to be scorched, singed, roasted, and finally eaten up by fire. It doesn't stop there: after Apophis is defeated, his allies and their families must meet the same fate.

SERQET, THE SCORPION GODDESS

Serqet is instantly identifiable by her scorpion-like features, including beady black eyes and sometimes a set of mandibles. She wears a scorpion on her head like a crown, and is faithfully followed by legions of scorpions.

You don't want to get on her bad side, but like many ferocious deities, Serqet is also capable of good. Since she has power over snakes, reptiles, and poisonous animals, Serqet is often called upon to protect and rescue people from deadly bites and stings. The Egyptian deserts are home to many snakes and scorpions, so it's no wonder that Ancient Egyptians considered her an important goddess to have on their side; some even worshipped her.

SOBEK, THE CROCODILE GOD

Sobek appears as a giant man with the head of a crocodile, or sometimes just as a crocodile. And he can act a lot like a crocodile when he wants to: traveling through water undetected, sneaking up on his prey, and dragging them underwater to drown. He can also channel powerful jets of water through his staff to force back his enemies or summon other crocodiles to do his dirty work.

He tries to thwart Carter and Sadie at every turn, but not everyone believed that he was all bad. Some say that he worked to repair Set's evil and protect the dead in the underworld. Ancient Egyptians who lived in areas where there were dangerous crocodiles worshipped him. In the city of Crocodilopolis, people even kept crocodiles in pools and adorned them with jewels to honor Sobek.

SWITCHBLADE DEMONS

In some of their tightest spots, Carter and Sadie encounter demons with knife blades in their heads. When they discover the Red Pyramid, switchblade demons are part of a huge demon army assembled by Set to protect it.

SERPOPARDS

Serpopards, sometimes known as longnecks, are creatures of chaos controlled by Set. They look a lot like cats—cats with long, scaly, green necks that have forked tongues and can spit

◀ This carving on the Narmer Palette shows two serpopards on leashes.

poison, that is. Two serpopards attack Carter, Sadie, Philip, and Khufu at Amos's mansion. They defeat Philip and Khufu but are then beaten when Muffin transforms into Bast. She ties their long necks together in a knot before slashing their heads off with her magic knives, dissolving them into dust.

THE SET ANIMAL

The Set animal doesn't have a proper name (and isn't very happy when Carter decides to start calling him Leroy) or look like any one creature. In ancient drawings, the Set animal often appears as a dog with a forked tail and square ears, but when it's chasing you, it's much scarier—imagine a greyhound the size of a horse with legs as long as its body, a long tail that has a mind of its own, ears that rotate, an anteater's snout, and razor-sharp teeth. The Set animal does Set's bidding and is as cunning and evil as its master. Once it catches the scent of its prey, the animal will stop at nothing to hunt it down.

Set animal, or jackal? ▶

SPHINX

Sphinxes are fearsome guardians of tombs and temples and their likenesses are found in Egypt and all over the world.

There are non-Egyptian sphinx myths, too, but all cultures agree on one thing: sphinxes are incredibly wise. Well known for their riddles, sphinxes reward those who solve them and punish those who can't come up with the right answer. A double sphinx called the Aker is the guardian of the entrance and exit to the Duat, or underworld. Those who answer her riddle correctly can pass the gates, but this treacherous sphinx shows no mercy to those who don't: she eats them on the spot.

They're most often shown with a lion's body and the head of a human wearing a headdress, but some sphinxes have the heads of a ram, hawk, or even the Set monster.

◀ The most famous sphinx in the world is the Great Sphinx at Giza, near Cairo, Egypt.

Different sphinxes have different names:

ANDROSPHINX: ***has the body of a lion and a human head***
CRIOSPHINX: ***has the body of a lion and the head of a ram***
HIEROCOSPHINX: ***has the body of a lion and the head of a falcon or hawk***

THE GRIFFIN

With the body of a lion and the head, wings, and talons of an eagle, griffins have the combined power of the king of the beasts and the king of the birds. Griffins are powerful magical guardians and often protect treasure. The Egyptians thought they were a sacred animal of Horus, which is why Carter can communicate with Freak the Griffin.

The griffin is associated with both Horus and his mortal enemy, Set, perhaps because it is a vicious hunter and a desert creature (Set's territory).

SECTION FOUR

HIEROGLYPHS, SYMBOLS & COMMANDS

THE KANE CHRONICLES SURVIVAL GUIDE

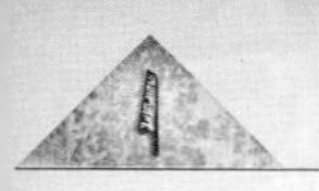

Speaking in Pictures

The ancient Egyptians used picture symbols called hieroglyphs to communicate with one another. Some hieroglyphs look like pictures of creatures, and others are more like odd-looking squiggles. Each symbol can represent a sound, a word, or an idea, and sometimes all three.

Today, very few people can read this ancient form of writing. Julius is an expert at translating even the most complicated hieroglyphics into English, both from years of learning and from using his magic. Much to her surprise, Sadie learns that without any prior experience, she's as skilled as her father at recognizing and reading hieroglyphics—a true natural. There are lots of different versions of hieroglyphs. Here is one guide to the equivalent of our alphabet.

Use this guide to write your name in hieroglyphs

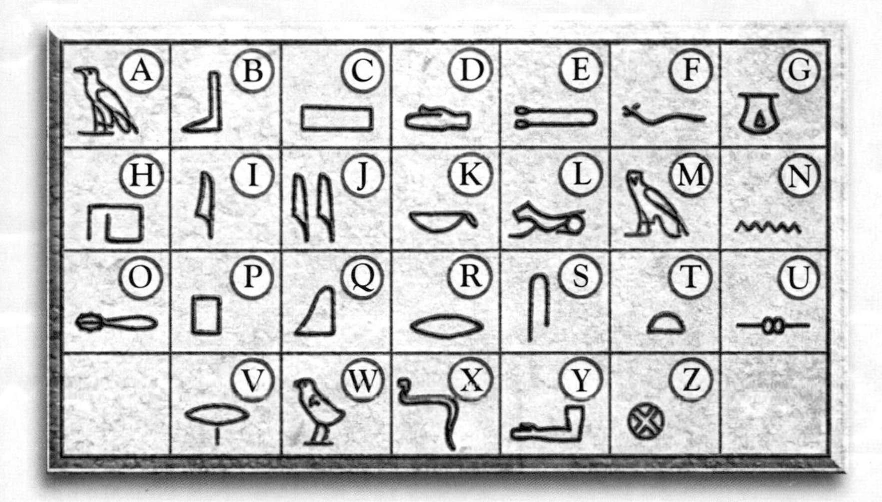

Decipher these hieroglyphs to discover Set's secret name. (But don't ever tell him who told you.)

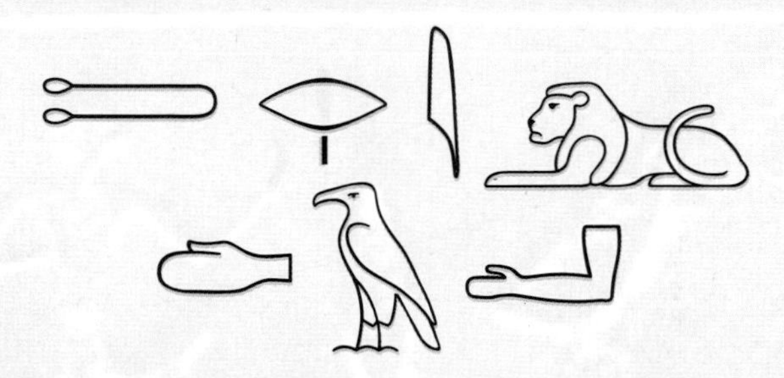

Symbols and Spells

Signs and symbols are everywhere. The Ancient Egyptians used symbols to represent the gods, for spells and incantations, and even wore them for protection. Carter and Sadie become familiar with a lot of ancient symbols and put them to good use in their adventures.

The *wedjat* eye is a human eye and eyebrow with some of the markings of a falcon's head. Known as the Eye of Horus (see page 41), it was first used as an amulet when Horus fashioned a *wedjat* eye and offered it to Osiris, who was restored to life by the amulet's power. Ever since, the symbol has been renowned for its power to restore life and protect against evil, which is why Julius chose it to be his son Carter's amulet.

This is the knot of the goddess Isis (see page 38) called the *tyet*. It looks like the knot in a sash of a robe, and since knots are often used to bind and release magic, there is a lot of power in this protective symbol. The *tyet* appears on the protective amulet that Sadie wears, which was also a gift from Julius.

The *ankh* looks a lot like a *tyet*, except its arms shoot straight out rather than curling downward. It was Ruby's favorite and is one of the most popular Egyptian symbols, and for good reason: an *ankh* is a symbol of life. Egyptian gods are often shown carrying *ankhs*. When a god holds an *ankh* to someone's lips, it means they are offering the breath of life, or the breath the person might need in the afterlife. The symbol for the House of Life is an *ankh* with a box around the top.

The *djed* is a column with four parallel bars across the top, and is a symbol for stability. Ancient Egyptians believed it was based on a man's backbone, Osiris's backbone, or a tree trunk with the branches cut off. Julius Kane wears a *djed* as his amulet, and Carter and Sadie later use it to call potential magicians to them.

A *ba* is the part of the soul that represents a person's personality and everything that makes them unique. A *ba* can act as a guardian, travel through time and space, and venture into the Duat. When Carter and Sadie dream, their *bas* often leave their sleeping bodies and visit other places. The symbol of the *ba* is a bird with a human head.

The *uraeus* is a symbol of royalty and kingship that first appeared in the Story of Ra, which is why this rearing, spitting cobra was once called "the fiery eye of Ra." In ancient times, the *uraeus* was thought to protect the kings, and they often adorned the crowns of pharaohs. As a hieroglyph, the *uraeus* usually represents a cobra.

SPOKEN AND DRAWN SPELLS

Magicians use spells to make things happen. When they speak a spell, blue or gold hieroglyphs appear to burn in the air for a moment before fading. Here are some magician's favorites and their meanings:

HI-NEHM
meaning "join" or "mend"

HA-DI
meaning "destroy"

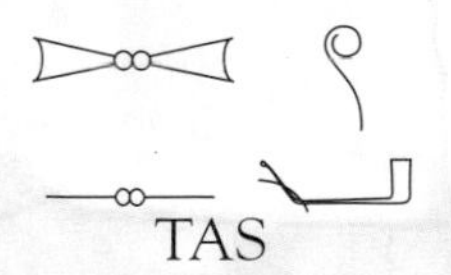

TAS
meaning "tie up" or "cocoon"

HA-WI
meaning "strike"

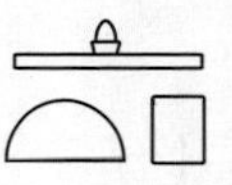

HA-TEP
meaning "be at peace"

A'MAX
meaning "burn"

N'DAH
meaning "protect"

L-MUN
meaning "hide"

CREATE YOUR OWN MAGICAL WORD SPELL

CARTER AND SADIE LEARN HOW TO CREATE THEIR OWN SPELLS, USING WORDS AND SYMBOLS, AND THE MORE THEY PRACTICE, THE BETTER CARTER AND SADIE GET AT PERFORMING MAGIC: STASHING ITEMS IN THE DUAT, CREATING PORTALS, AND DEFEATING MONSTERS. IF YOU'RE AN ASPIRING MAGICIAN, LEARNING HOW TO CREATE SPELLS IS AN ABSOLUTE MUST.

HERE ARE THE RULES.

1. Spells can be written in any language, but hieroglyphs are best because they are the language of magic.

2. If you draw a symbol for a living being, it is important not to draw a whole creature, or the magic you channel might bring

"CARTER DREW A SIMPLE HIEROGLYPH OF A BIRD. THE PICTURE WRIGGLED, PEELED ITSELF OFF THE PAPYRUS, AND FLEW AWAY. IT SPLATTERED CARTER'S HEAD WITH SOME HIEROGLYPH DROPPINGS ON ITS WAY OUT. I COULDN'T HELP LAUGHING AT CARTER'S EXPRESSION."

—SADIE

it to life (Carter didn't know this, which got him into a sticky situation). For example, make sure you leave a wing off a bird or a leg off a cat, unless you want all sorts of animals scampering through your house.

3. Magic can be very powerful indeed, so be careful what you wish for.

The symbols you draw will summon that particular object or creature from the Ma'at, which is the creative power of the universe. To get started, you'll need a papyrus scroll (or roll of paper) and a stylus (Egyptian pen), or modern equivalents. If your hieroglyphs come to life from the page, you'll know that you're a modern magician.

COULD YOU BE A MODERN MAGICIAN? FIND SOME PENS AND PAPER AND SEE WHAT YOU CAN SUMMON.

SECTION FIVE

EXPLORING THE HOUSE OF LIFE

THE KANE CHRONICLES SURVIVAL GUIDE

The House of Life

The headquarters of the House of Life is in Egypt, deep beneath the city of Cairo. It is the oldest branch of the House of Life and serves as a home and training ground for magicians.

The House has always been led by a Chief Lector, who was the pharaoh's head magician in ancient times. Reporting to the Chief Lector are senior magicians called Sem priests. They are the oldest and most powerful members of the House, overseeing the world's 360 nomes, or regions. Senior magicians supervise scribes, the rank-and-file magicians who can summon magic by writing and saying magical words.

Carter and Sadie first enter the House through a sand tunnel portal, led by Zia Rashid. She takes them down an interminable staircase that ends on the edge of a deep chasm, with a single wooden plank as a bridge. More scares await: two jackal-headed warriors with crossed spears guard the doorway on the other side.

JOURNEY THROUGH THE HOUSE OF LIFE

Zia, Carter, and Sadie pass through a vast market with stalls selling boomerang wands, animated clay dolls, cobras, scrolls, and glittering amulets. They peep into a scrying school, where children learn to see what is happening in other nomes by looking into bowls of oil. They reach a massive set of bronze doors with fires on either side, behind which is the Hall of Ages.

The Hall of Ages

The Hall of Ages is at the heart of the First Nome, and shows those who walk through it memories of Egyptian history. Every year it grows a little longer as it records the recent past. Carter and Sadie are stunned by its size: it's as big as a football field and supported by massive stone pillars. The room shines with a shimmering blue carpet, floating balls of fire, and tiny hieroglyphs floating in the air.

CHIEF LECTOR ISKANDAR

Iskandar is ancient (around 2,000 years old) and prefers to speak in his birth tongue of Alexandrian Greek. He was the last magician to be trained before Egypt fell to Rome and the House of Life was forced underground. Although the Chief Lector is the master of the House of Life, he doesn't sit on the throne at the end of the Hall of Ages. As his role is to serve and protect the pharaoh, he faithfully keeps the vacant throne ready for the return of the pharaohs.

MICHEL DESJARDINS

Desjardins acts as the aged Chief Lector's spokesman and is hostile to the Kanes when they come to meet Iskandar. Desjardins claims not to hold Sadie and Carter responsible for the crimes of their father, who broke a sacred law of the House of Life that forbids

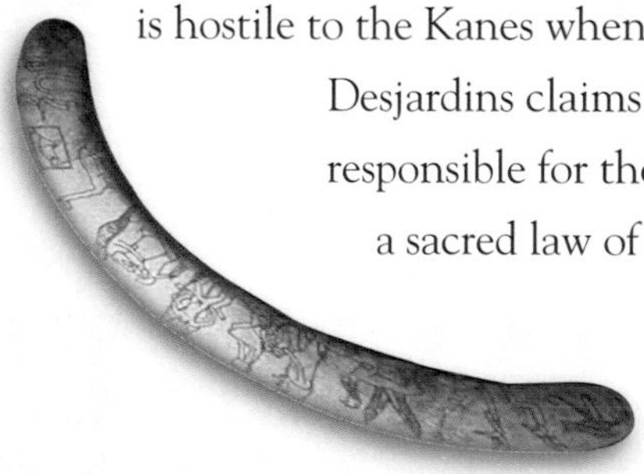

◀ Magic wand

mortals from summoning the gods. And he broke it twice: first at Cleopatra's Needle when Ruby died and Bast was released, and again when he used the Rosetta Stone to release five powerful gods.

Iskandar and Desjardins want Carter and Sadie to stay in the First Nome, where they will be under its protection—and where the magicians will be able to determine just how powerful the Kane siblings are and whether they pose a threat to the House.

Q: Where is the Three-hundred-and-sixtieth (and last) Nome?

A: Antarctica, and it's a punishment nome. Nothing there but some cold magicians and magic penguins. Better not offend the Chief Lector!

ZIA RASHID

Zia had a happy childhood living with her family on the banks of the Nile. Her life turned upside down after her father brought home a small red stone statue of a monster and accidentally unleashed its power. The monster destroyed the entire village and everyone in it—except for young Zia. Chief Lector Iskandar rescued her, and she became a scribe in the First Nome.

Carter and Sadie first glimpse Zia in London, when they are with their father at Cleopatra's Needle, but they don't discover her identity until they're in New York, running from Serqet and her scorpion army. To escape, they run into the Temple of Dendur in the Metropolitan Museum of Art, where Zia opens the portal to the House of Life.

Zia's magical skills

Zia carries a plain wooden rod that is anything but ordinary: it turns into a long black staff, topped with a carved lion's head, from which she conjures flames and spells.

With the help of her trusty staff and years of training, Zia demonstrates impressive magical skills to ward off Serqet, defeating her with the Seven Ribbons of Hathor, red ribbons that come to life and wrap and burn the scorpion goddess.

Later, she helps Carter and Sadie trick and defeat the goddess Sekhmet. They persuade the goddess in her lioness form to drink gallons of hot salsa, telling her that it is blood, which turns her into a giant sleepy cow (see The Stories of Ra, page 30).

VLADIMIR MENSHIKOV

Vladimir Menshikov, nicknamed Vlad the Inhaler, heads the Eighteenth Nome in Russia. He claims to be descended from the god Ra, and one of most powerful magicians in the world.

Menshikov is an ally of Michel Desjardins, and both magicians fear that Carter and Sadie have upset the balance of Ma'at by awakening the gods and teaching forbidden magic. For this reason, they don't want Carter and Sadie to succeed in their plan to restore Ra to his throne to prevent Apophis from rising. Menshikov attempts to keep Carter and Sadie from finding the Book of Ra, and he's not afraid to use dangerous dark magic.

Vlad's dangerous spells: Sympathetic magic and execration

When magicians perform sympathetic magic, they bind together two connected things—one small and one large—to make them work together. This type of magic is advanced, and not many magicians attempt these spells. The more similar the two items are, the better the binding works. Vlad uses sympathetic magic to bind a corkscrew-headed demon called Death-to-Corks to an actual corkscrew.

But Vlad doesn't stop at sympathetic magic. He goes a step further to perform execration, which allows him to destroy the larger object (in the corkscrew case, the hapless demon) by breaking the smaller one (the corkscrew). Execration can be used for good, but Vlad execrates the demon to generate the energy to summon Set, a major god, which is forbidden by the House of Life.

"If done right, most victims didn't stand a chance. Regular mortals, magicians, ghosts, even demons could be wiped off the face of the earth. Execration might not destroy major powers like gods, but it would still be like detonating a nuclear bomb in their face. They'd be blasted so deep into the Duat, they might never come back."

—Carter

LIBRARY
No. 0324424
This book belongs to:
CAIRO MUSEUM of ANTIQUITIES
Midan El Tahrir, Cairo
Title: Ancient Egypt
A Brief History
BORROWER'S NAME
DATE DUE
JUN 03
JUN 15
Z. Rashid
AUG 07
AUG 28
C. Kane
SEP 30

THE ANCIENT TIMES COLLECTION

ANCIENT EGYPT

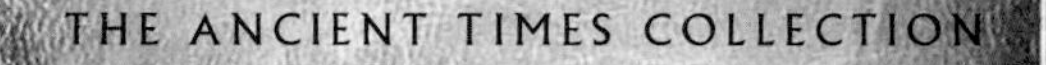

A Brief History

ANCIENT EGYPT
AND ITS RULERS

Thousands of years ago, the country of Egypt in northeast Africa was divided into two parts. The southern lands around the great River Nile were known as Upper Egypt. The northern lands were called Lower Egypt. The symbol of Upper Egypt was a vulture, which eats dead animals. The symbol of Lower Egypt was the cobra, a deadly snake. These two animals became symbols of royal power.

About 5,000 years ago both regions came together as one country, ruled by a pharaoh called King Narmer.

Pharaohs lived in grand palaces. They had many

religious duties. The queen and royal family lived at the royal court with nobles, top priests, officials, and army leaders. These were the most powerful people in the country.

Most pharaohs were men, but one woman did rule as pharaoh. Her name was Hatshepsut, and she ruled for about 20 years. At that time Egyptian women could own property and hold official positions and had much more freedom than women in other ancient cultures.

Hidden Hair

No one was allowed to see the hair of a pharaoh. He always covered his head with a crown or headdress. When he appeared at an important event or ceremony, he wore a false beard to show he was king.

Carter and Sadie saw some of these events as they walked through the Hall of Ages.

B.C.E.

3500
People settle in Nile valley

3100
First hieroglyphs drawn; King Narmer unites Upper and Lower Egypt

2600
Pyramids of Giza built

2055
Pharaoh Mentuhotep II rules all Egypt

1473
Hatshepsut becomes pharaoh

1333
Tutankhamun becomes pharaoh

1274
Pharaoh Ramesses II defeats the Hittites in the Battle of Kadesh (below)

1100
Upper and Lower Egypt split into two states

728
Nubian king Piye conquers Egypt

671
Assyrians attack Egypt

525
Persians conquer Egypt

332
Alexander the Great conquers Egypt

305
Ptolemy I becomes pharaoh

196
Rosetta Stone carved

30
Romans annex Egypt

C.E.

642
Arabs conquer Egypt

1517
Ottoman Turks invade

1798
Napoleon Bonaparte occupies Egypt

1799
Rosetta Stone found

1822
Hieroglyphs are deciphered

1859–1869
Suez Canal built

1922
Howard Carter (after whom Carter was named) discovers tomb of Tutankhamun

Mummies

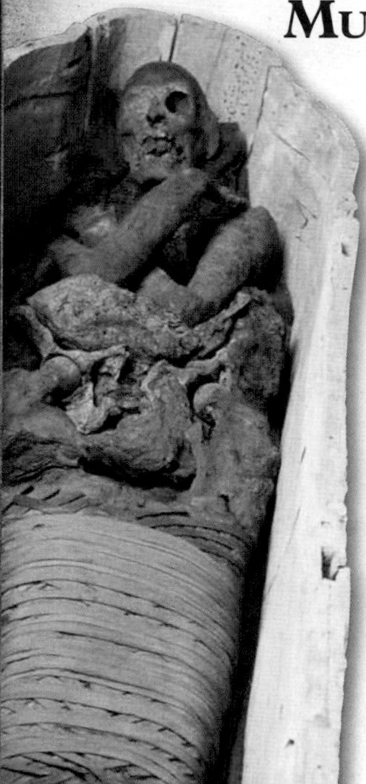

Mummies are instantly recognizable today as horror movie monsters and Halloween costume fodder. But back in Ancient Egyptian times, mummification was taken very seriously: important Egyptians were made into mummies to prepare them for their new existence in the afterlife.

The process took a long time and cost quite a bit, so the honor was reserved for pharaohs and the very wealthy. First, specially trained priests would ritually clean and purify the body. Then they pulled the brain out through the nose with long hooks (it wasn't a pretty process). After that, the corpse was left to dry for forty days; then the priests rubbed it with oil and stuffed it with packing.

Once all that was done, the priests would put protective amulets, gold, and jewels on the body and wrap the fingers, toes, arms, and legs in layers of linen. They covered the head with a mask, and if the person was rich enough, they would place the entire body in an ornate coffin shaped and painted like a body. With the mummy now ready for burial, the priests held a procession to take it to a tomb, laying the mummy to rest there for all eternity.

Pet Mummies

There were even animal mummies! Many different kinds of animal mummies have been discovered, from cats and dogs to exotic animals, like monkeys, lizards, and crocodiles. By keeping their pets with them, Egyptians gained companions in the afterlife, and honored the god of each particular animal.

PYRAMID TOMBS

While many pharaohs were laid to rest in square tombs in the Valley of the Kings, some were entombed inside great pyramids. Inside the huge stone monuments, the dead pharaoh was surrounded by food, possessions, and *shabti* servants to look after him in the next life.

The Great Pyramid at Giza

The most famous pyramid in the world is in a city called Giza, the tomb of King Khufu. It was no easy task to build such a grand structure—it took thousands of workers many years to complete. Just to get the massive stone blocks to the site, they had to float them on barges down the Nile. Then they put the blocks on wooden sleds and dragged them through the desert, built ramps to haul the blocks up, and stacked them one level at a time. When they pulled down the ramps, they left a magnificent triangular pyramid behind.

A Massive Achievement
In its prime, the pyramid stood 482 feet high, making it the tallest building on Earth for thousands of years. All without the convenience of modern machinery!

WHAT HAPPENED TO TUT?

Tutankhamun was only nine or ten when he became pharaoh. He didn't do much in his ten-year reign, so history forgot about ol' King Tut until his treasure-filled tomb was excavated in 1922. The tomb's artifacts have since been seen by millions, making Tut famous. The cause of his death is one of history's greatest mysteries. Some think that he was murdered by a greedy friend, a power-hungry deputy, or rebellious servants. Others say that Tut died after a chariot accident or from an infection, but we'll likely never know the truth.

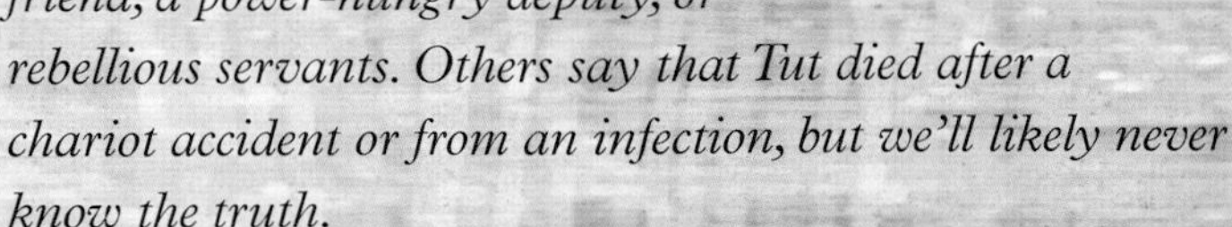

SECTION SIX
WELCOME TO THE
TWENTY-FIRST
NOME
THE KANE CHRONICLES SURVIVAL GUIDE

The Twenty-first Nome

A Tour of the Twenty-first Nome

Greetings! I am your guide* shabti *to the magical headquarters of Amos Kane in the Twenty-first Nome. *For those of you who are wondering,* shabtis *are magical models of slaves that are put into the tombs of the pharaohs to help them in the afterlife. But that's not all we do....*

This glorious mansion becomes Carter and Sadie's home when they live with Amos. He set up his HQ in Brooklyn, east of New York City's Hudson and East rivers, to follow an ancient Egyptian tradition. Living on the west side of the Nile was considered bad luck because it was the side where the Egyptians buried their dead. The east bank of the Nile was the side of the living, the side the sun rose, and was favored by Ra.

We start the tour in the Great Room. Note the majestic cedar beams and the many displays of Egyptian musical instruments and weapons. Look up to the balconies and view the wrap-around terrace through these glass panels.

Please do not roll on the snakeskin rug—you can tell by its size that it came from no ordinary serpent, and its magical properties can be harmful. The black marble statue of Thoth towering over us is thirty feet tall. Please do not touch.

Next we will briefly visit the library. As you see, the doors are marked with the Eye of Horus. Stand back please; there are three sets of stairs leading down. Gaze upon the ceiling to see the goddess of the sky, Nut. On the floor, her husband Geb, god of the earth, reclines, just as in the outside world. Every hole in the wall holds a papyrus scroll, but do not touch—many have injurious charms attached.

▲ Thoth as a baboon

Now, if you will come this way, Khufu and Philip of Macedonia are waiting for us on the terrace.

Khufu is our resident baboon. As you know, both the god Thoth and the moon god Khonsu sometimes appear as baboons, though I'm fairly certain that Khufu is just your average, run-of-the-mill, walking, serving, outwitting baboon. He sure does eat a lot, though. Khufu is particularly fond of any food ending in "o"; feel free to offer anything you may have along these lines. And if any of you would like to polish up your basketball skills, Khufu would be delighted to play....

A mangO is one of Khufu's favorite treats ▶

Khufu

Come over to the swimming pool and say hello to Philip. As you'll see, he is a rare albino crocodile, but please don't refer to his hue, as he is most sensitive about it. Don't worry—even though his teeth are enormous, he prefers bacon to human, so you're quite safe. Unless, of course, he senses that you present a threat to the House of Life and the Twenty-first Nome in particular. Then you're in trouble.

On the bottom of Philip's pool you'll see some elaborate decorations—very similar to those in his family's pool in Crocodilopolis. Seeing them every day probably stops Philip from feeling homesick here in New York.

You'd like to see Carter and Sadie's quarters? Alas, they're off saving the world, and I wouldn't dare enter without permission. So this

is the end of today's tour. Souvenir amulets are available, and for those who were unable to resist the library scrolls, one of our trainee magicians is waiting with a very reasonably priced charm-reversal kit by the elevator.

SECTION SEVEN
CARTER & SADIE'S
TRAINEE
MAGICIANS
THE KANE CHRONICLES SURVIVAL GUIDE

The Trainee Magicians

Defeating the forces of evil and resurrecting a centuries-dead deity isn't the kind of job you want to do alone, so Carter and Sadie send out a *djed* amulet that draws kids with magical potential to their headquarters. They train these recruits to help them fight the forces of chaos.

WALT STONE

Walt is fourteen and traveled cross-country from Seattle to answer Carter and Sadie's call. He was the first to arrive and soon proved to be a talented charm-maker. The many gold neck chains he wears are much more than jewelry: they're homemade magical amulets with strong protective properties.

"I don't know what it is about him, but he has a sort of gravity that draws the group's attention when he's about to speak."—Sadie

JAZ

Jaz was another early arrival at headquarters. She is a pretty, blond, and likeable cheerleader from Nashville, nice to everyone and always ready to help. Her talent is healing magic, so she's great to have around if something goes wrong, which happens to Carter and Sadie all too often. Jaz carries a sturdy bag decorated with an image of her patron, the lion goddess Sekhmet.

Jaz's magic at the Brooklyn Museum

When Carter and Sadie are trying to escape from the Brooklyn Museum, Jaz creates a circle of magic energy that controls the vicious plague spirits and sets fire to everything, allowing everyone to escape safely; but she draws on all of her stores of magic to protect her friends.

Jaz's healing charm

Jaz gives Sadie a charm to help Carter. It's a healing statue, used to expel sickness or curses, and meant to heal a specific person—Carter, should he be in a life-and-death situation. Jaz gives the statue Carter's hair, features, and his sword, and writes his name in hieroglyphs on its chest. But she doesn't tell Sadie how or when she should use it. . . .

Other trainees

There are eighteen other trainees who travel from all over the world to join Carter, Sadie, Walt, and Jaz. A handful are old enough to go to college, but most are aged between nine and fifteen. Among them are Felix, the baby of the bunch at nine years old; Julien, from Boston; Alyssa, from Carolina; Sean, from Dublin; and Cleo, from Rio de Janeiro. The blood of the pharaohs runs through each of their veins (which is about the only thing they have in common), giving them a natural capacity for magic and for hosting the gods.

Magical Specialties

Every magician has natural talents that indicate their specialties. If any of these seem familiar, you might want to hop a portal and join the trainees.

DIVINER

Knowing what the future holds can lead magicians to attempt dangerous feats in order to change it. But if you're a diviner who has seen something awful, you probably already know that. . . .

ANIMAL CHARMER

It may sound unimportant, but animal charming has always been a powerful and useful skill. After all, when dangerous creatures will do your bidding, you can make your enemies squirm, or help your friends out of a bind. Finding a cobra in your bed is a definite sign that you've offended an animal charmer.

ELEMENTALIST

Elementalists can control the five basic elements: earth, fire, air, water, and cheese! A good elementalist can summon the forces of nature to launch devastating attacks.

COMBAT MAGICIAN

Combat magicians don't enter battles in their own bodies. They use fearsome avatars, which wrap the user in magical armor and allow them to pound and smash their opponents to smithereens. This is powerful magic and requires a great deal of stamina and strength. If you like the idea of becoming a magical juggernaut who can smash through walls and wade through armies, this is the discipline for you.

NECROMANCER

These skilled magicians can summon spirits of the dead to answer questions, perform tasks, or haunt people's dreams (so don't get a necromancer angry). Spirits were important forces in Ancient Egypt, and the necromancer can use or ward them off as needed. Necromancy is a good skill to have, as long as you're not afraid of ghosts.

HEALER

Healing is a very popular and respected discipline, so if you've got the healing touch, perhaps you can become a *sunu*, or healer. Magic was the medicine of ancient times, and magicians were called upon to cure all sorts of wounds and diseases, so it's not a field for the squeamish.

CHARM-MAKERS

The *sau*, or charm-makers, are magical craftsmen who know how to make amulets, rings, and other powerful charms. They aren't always the fastest in combat, but they can make incredible tools to help in a fight. People who are good with their hands and like designing magic items should consider studying charm-making.

PATH OF THE GODS

In the time of the Ancient Egyptians, magicians learned to draw power directly from an Egyptian deity. For instance, a combat magician might draw on the power of Horus, the god of war, to be unbeatable in battle; or a healer might call on Serqet to cure a particularly tricky scorpion sting. The ultimate goal was to become the "eye" of the god—a perfect combination of mortal will and godly

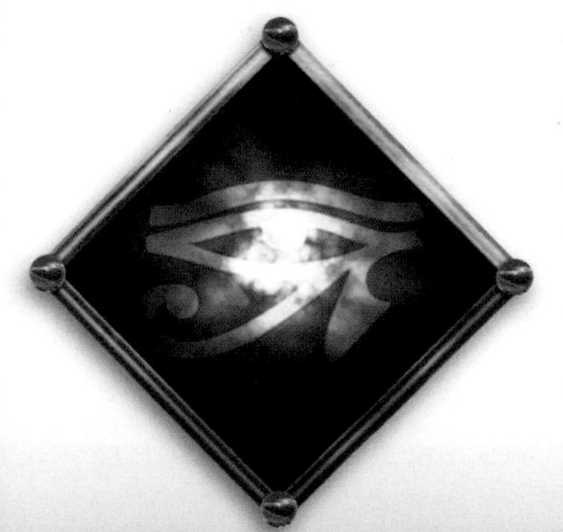

power. The drawback is that the gods are unpredictable and can use mortals as their tools, which is why studying the path of the gods is now forbidden. This is dangerous magic that could get you in lots of trouble!

MAGICAL DOWNSIDES

Magic doesn't always make things easier. Carter and Sadie learn that there are drawbacks, like having a spell fail or backfire, worrying about someone else using magic against you, needing to don the linen clothing that magicians are supposed to wear (mortal clothes and fabrics can interfere with channeling magic). So think long and hard before you join the trainees—you might find the risk outweighs the reward.

The Kanes' Mission

Carter and Sadie decide they need to recruit help after their battle with Set at the Red Pyramid. They realize that Set intends to continue his attempts to release Apophis, no matter what they do.

—∞—

So the Kanes set out to train new magicians to help in their mission to prevent Apophis from escaping. They need to find and unite the three parts of the Book of Ra and restore Ra to his former glory. This is, they believe, the only way to prevent the world from ending, as it is predicted to do if Apophis escapes and tries to destroy Ma'at (the order of the universe).

—∞—

They must stop him before the spring equinox, when the forces of chaos and Ma'at can be tipped one way or the other. Unfortunately, the equinox is also the perfect time for Apophis to escape . . . .

Carter and Sadie battling demons

SECTION EIGHT

GUIDE TO MAGICAL PLACES

THE KANE CHRONICLES SURVIVAL GUIDE

Locations of Power

Interested in magic? Then consider this your guidebook to places protected by ancient spells that you absolutely must visit.

EGYPTIAN OBELISKS

The three Egyptian obelisks, each known as Cleopatra's Needle, have a strong pull for magicians. They are made of red granite and engraved with hieroglyphs. Each is located in a major city and is a popular tourist destination (especially for magician tourists).

1. The London Needle

This obelisk was made in 1450 B.C.E. It was one of a pair found in Heliopolis, Egypt, and given to the British as a gift in 1819. But the obelisk didn't come to London until 1877 (it takes some planning to transport a 224-ton obelisk from country to country). It made the journey inside a huge iron cylinder towed by a ship.

London

On the way, the cylinder capsized during a storm, but it managed to stay afloat and reach London safely.

A time capsule was hidden beneath the London obelisk.

Among the items inside were a map of London, ten newspapers, a box of cigars, a small bronze model of the monument, a set of British coins, a rupee, a portrait of Queen Victoria, and twelve photographs of the world's most beautiful women.

2. The New York Needle

The second obelisk of the pair found in Heliopolis can be found in New York City's Central Park. It was transported to the U.S. in 1880, carried in the hold of a steamship. When it arrived, it took thirty-two pairs of horses to drag the obelisk from the Hudson River into the park!

3. The Paris Needle

The Paris obelisk is one of a pair that once stood by the entrance to the Luxor Temple. The second obelisk is still in its original position in Egypt. The Paris needle was raised in 1833, making it the first of the three needles to find a new home. Beautifully landscaped, the Paris needle has fountains on either side.

Paris

THE SITE OF THE RED PYRAMID

Sadie and Carter travel cross-country to discover this magical pyramid that Set built in a cavern under Camelback Mountain. The mountain is the biggest landmark in Phoenix Valley, Arizona. The shape of Camelback Mountain closely resembles the hump and head of a kneeling camel, which is how it got its name. Apart from this, the Egyptian connection is not entirely clear to mortals.

MUSEUMS

1. The British Museum, London

Museums are important places for magicians, especially if they contain Egyptian artifacts, as the British Museum does. Since Julius Kane is a highly respected Egyptologist, he has no problem taking Sadie and Carter on a tour of the Egyptian wing, and he even manages to persuade the curator to leave them alone with the Rosetta Stone (some magic might have been involved). This

amazing slab was carved in the year 196 B.C.E., but the language was lost over time. Many scholars worked on deciphering the hieroglyphs on the stone, but it wasn't translated until 1822, when French Egyptologist Jean-François Champollion discovered their meaning, which made the stone even more special. The words carved into the stone were written by priests to honor the Egyptian Pharaoh, and list all the good things that the Pharaoh had done for the priests and the people of Egypt, giving valuable insight into Egyptian history.

2. The Hermitage Museum, Moscow

Carter and Sadie visit Moscow with Bes while searching for a section of the Book of Ra, and they meet Vlad Menshikov when they visit the Hermitage Museum. The museum has the best Egyptian collection in Russia, and the headquarters of the Eighteenth Nome is rumored to be inside it.

3. The Metropolitan Museum of Art, New York

This is another key site for magicians and the gods. It's near the New York obelisk to which Bast, Carter, and Sadie flee when Amos's headquarters comes under attack. To escape from Serqet the scorpion goddess, Bast tells Sadie and Carter to flee to the Egyptian temple inside the museum, where they will be able to create a portal.

An Egyptian Temple in New York

The Temple of Dendur is a real Egyptian temple, which now stands in the United States. It was built around 15 B.C.E. on the west bank of the Nile River and dedicated to Isis and Osiris.

When the Egyptians built a dam across the Nile, creating Lake Nasser, they moved the temple and gave it to the United States.

Temple Facts

- 642 sandstone blocks
- in total, blocks weigh more than 800 tons
- packed into 661 crates and shipped to the United States
- temple given to the Metropolitan Museum of Art in New York in 1967

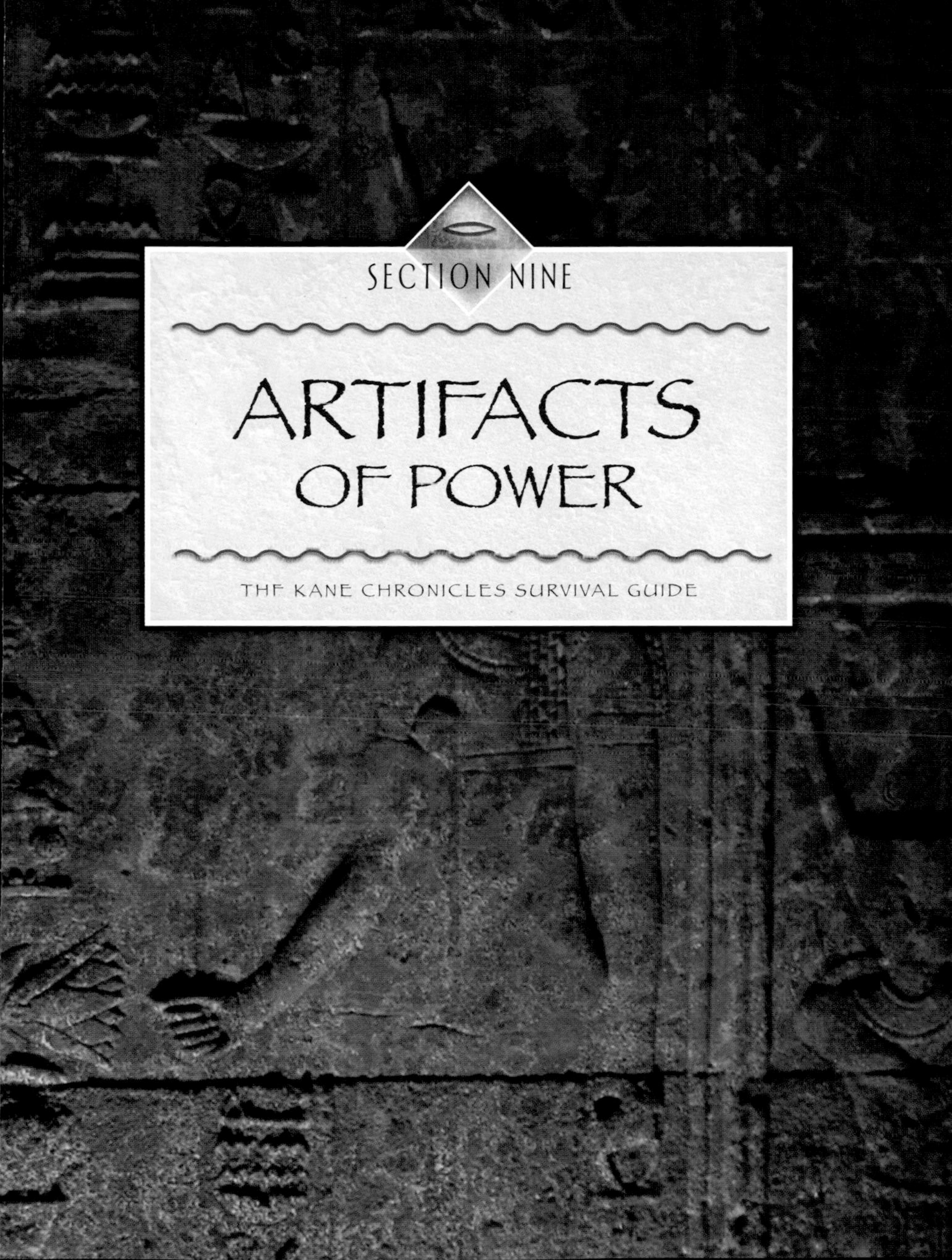
SECTION NINE
ARTIFACTS
OF POWER
THE KANE CHRONICLES SURVIVAL GUIDE

Sources of Power

In search of a good read? Or maybe a spell to vanquish demons? Well, read on. . . .

MAGICAL BOOKS

The Book of Ra

The Book of Ra was a powerful magical scroll that Ra's priests created to call upon Ra in the event of a major catastrophe. Not wanting it to fall into the wrong hands, the priests divided it into three sections and hid each scroll separately, knowing that only a worthy magician would be able to find them and reawaken the sun god.

Ra has lain dormant for many years, but Carter and Sadie need his help, and the Book of Ra is their only hope. As the natural enemy of Apophis, the god of Chaos, who is threatening to escape from his weakening prison, Ra is the only one who can keep Apophis from destroying Ma'at (the order of the universe) and plunging the earth into endless darkness.

The Book of Overcoming Apophis

Sadie and Carter find this scroll in Amos's library in the Twenty-first Nome, but they don't realize its significance right away.
For more, see page 55.

Blood of the Pharaohs
Carter and Sadie make another great find in the library: a scroll that lists all the dynasties in Ancient Egypt, called *Blood of the Pharaohs*. Here they find the cartouche encircling their family name, and learn the truth about their family's storied history and immense power.

WHAT IS A CARTOUCHE?
Ancient Egyptians believed that they could protect themselves in life and death by writing their name in hieroglyphs and drawing an oval ring around it, symbolizing magical protective ropes. This enclosure is called a cartouche.

The Book of the Dead
This ancient book guides its readers through the Duat and into the Land of the Dead. Rich Egyptians were buried with it so that they wouldn't get lost in the afterlife (the poor ones had to fend for themselves). When Carter and Sadie journey to the Land of the Dead in search of a feather of truth, their escort is guided by *The Book of the Dead*.

WEAPONS AND MAGICAL TOOLS

Khopesh

The *khopesh* is a sword made of bronze or iron that is designed to disarm an opponent by hooking his or her weapon. The blade is almost two feet long and sharp only on the outer edge of the curve. Egyptian soldiers wield a *khopesh* in one hand and a wicker shield in the other.

▲ Carter brandishes a *khopesh*

Staff

Along with wands, staffs are one of the two most important tools for a magician. Magicians can use their staffs to control the elements, summon spirits, conjure flames, or simply whack bad guys on the head. A staff can be turned into any number of helpful creatures, such as snakes, hippos, tigers, or crocodiles. Magicians use their staffs to fight enemies and protect innocents, but in the wrong hands, a staff can conjure an evil animal.

Wands

Egyptian wands are curved and made from hippo tusks split in half. A wand can be used to draw protective circles and cast healing spells, but also to combat enemies in many ways: from being thrown as weapons, to creating a magic shield.

Magician's box

Magicians always have to be prepared, so they keep their spell-casting supplies and magical aids with them at all times in a handy box. The tools inside vary according to its owner's preference, but may include papyrus, a stylus, and ink for writing scrolls; wax for making *shabti* statues; and any number of protective charms and amulets. If you need to travel light and have the skills, you can store your box in the Duat and access it whenever you need to.

▲ This ornate coffin shows King Tut with crook and flail

Crook and flail

These Egyptian symbols of power were used in all royal ceremonies and believed to have protective powers in the afterlife, which is why kings were almost always buried with crooks and flails.

Shabti

The word *shabti* means "answerer," so it's no wonder that this name was given to small statues that awaken only to answer the call of their masters. *Shabti* can be immensely useful to magicians in

need of help, so magicians are trained to make their own *shabti* figures to bring to life as needed.

In early Egypt, dead Egyptian kings were placed in elaborate tombs filled with all sorts of goodies, including painted boxes filled with *shabti* to carry out tasks for them in the underworld. One needy pharaoh was entombed with more than a thousand *shabti* by his side!

THE FEATHER OF TRUTH

"The feather cannot abide the smallest lie. If I gave it to you, and you spoke a single untruth while you carried it, or acted in a way that was not truthful, you would burn to ashes."—Anubis

When souls reach the afterlife, they can't just waltz right in: their heart has to be weighed against the feather of truth to measure their life against their lies. If the feather is lighter than their heart, it means that the person has done more bad than good and is not allowed to cross into the afterlife.

The feather of truth is incredibly important, but it is also enormously powerful and it can be used to defeat enemies. Carter and Sadie need a feather of truth in order to defeat Set, but whoever is in possession of one has to tell the truth at all times (or face the consequences). This means that Sadie has to be very careful to keep even the littlest white lie bottled up inside.

THE FEATHER-OF-TRUTH CHALLENGE

Think it's easy to tell the truth? Think again. Just how truthful would you be if you had to answer these questions in front of all your friends?

What's your . . .

- *most embarrassing story?*
- *grossest bad habit?*
- *deepest, darkest secret?*
- *biggest fear?*

If you can answer those questions honestly for all the world to hear, congratulations! You are worthy of possessing the feather of truth.

MAGICAL TIMES

Equinoxes

An equinox occurs on just two days of the year, when the day and the night are exactly the same length. When the hours of daylight and darkness are in perfect balance, Ra and Apophis are on an equal footing, so the forces of Chaos and Ma'at can be easily tipped one way or another. To help keep magicians and gods from tipping the scales, all the portals in the world shut down during the equinox, except at sunrise and sunset.

Solstices

Solstices are magical times because they mark either the shortest or longest day in a year. The dates depend on whether you live in the northern or southern hemisphere. In the northern hemisphere, the winter solstice falls in December and the summer solstice falls in June.

In Ancient Egypt the summer solstice was one of the most important times of the year, when the sun was at its highest and the Nile was beginning to rise. The Egyptians looked forward to this time, when the river flooded the land around it and the mud it left behind made their fields fertile. They held special ceremonies to honor the goddess Isis, believing that she was mourning her dead husband, Osiris, and that her tears made the Nile rise.

"The spring equinox. A powerful time for magic. The hours of day and night are exactly balanced, meaning the forces of Chaos and Ma'at can be easily tipped one way or the other. It's the perfect time to awaken Ra. In fact, it's our only chance until the fall equinox, six months from now. But we can't wait that long."—Bast

SECTION TEN

TRAVELING WITH THE KANES

Carter's and Sadie's Magical Journeys

Carter and Sadie go on a number of journeys, but not journeys as we know them. Many of their adventures begin and end at magic portals.

Magic portals and their uses
Gods and magicians use portals to instantly transport themselves to another part of the world. To open a portal, you need a magic artifact, which is why you often find portals at museums. Sadie's relic for opening portals in the Twenty-first Nome was a small stone sphinx from the ruins of Heliopolis.

There are rules for using portals. They cannot be used several times in quick succession. And they need to cool down between travelers. At an equinox, all the portals in the world shut down except at sunset and sunrise. Equinoxes happen in spring and autumn and are the two days each year when night and day are exactly the same length and therefore perfectly balanced.

Some places are tricky to teleport to, such as Alexandria in Egypt. It's where the Egyptian empire fell apart, so magic tends to get twisted. The only working portals are in the old city, under thirty feet of seawater!

Alexandria

Powerful curses can prevent portal travel—or make it difficult; the oasis at Bahariya in the Sahara, for example. Here there's a huge network of tunnels and chambers no one's opened in thousands of years, and perhaps ten thousand mummies.

The portal at Bahariya

Magical Boat Journeys

"Thoth, the god of knowledge, had once told us that we'd always have the power to summon a boat when we needed one, because we were the blood of the pharaohs."—Carter

The other form of magical transport Carter and Sadie use is an Egyptian boat. Amos transports them to New York in a matter of minutes, in a reed boat summoned by simply drawing a hieroglyph.

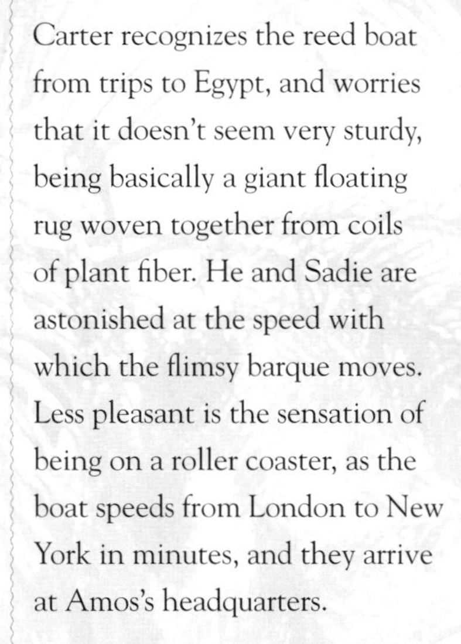

Carter recognizes the reed boat from trips to Egypt, and worries that it doesn't seem very sturdy, being basically a giant floating rug woven together from coils of plant fiber. He and Sadie are astonished at the speed with which the flimsy barque moves. Less pleasant is the sensation of being on a roller coaster, as the boat speeds from London to New York in minutes, and they arrive at Amos's headquarters.

Amos appears with the reed boat again after Carter, Sadie, and Bast summon Nephthys from the Rio Grande to help them fight Set, but find themselves set upon by Sobek, the crocodile god.

This time the boat takes to the skies as they fly off to Las Cruces to an encounter with Zia and Desjardins. Trying to stop the

Kanes from searching for Set, Desjardins summons Sekhmet. The avenging goddess pursues their sky boat until they crash-land in a huge pile of chilies, and Carter finds a clever way to turn Sekhmet into a giant sleeping cow. . . .

The pharaoh's barge

Carter and Sadie's second magical boat is the pharaoh's barge they sail down the River of Night that runs through the Duat, to search for Ra. At the start, the boat is a wreck, with a tattered sail, broken oars, and cobwebbed rigging. To make matters worse, it is haunted by specters in the form of Gran and Gramps Faust. Carter defeats them using his pharaoh's crook and flail, and he and Sadie journey through the twelve sections of the river, encountering a different challenge in each section, or house. Among these challenges are figuring out the secret name of Knum the ram god, searching Sunny Acres (the rest home of the gods) for Ra, and playing a deadly game of senet with Bes and Khonsu, the moon god. Eventually the boat takes them to their encounter with Apophis himself in the red cavern.

Approaching the Red Pyramid

"The world had changed.
The sun god had returned.
Apophis was free from his cage,
and although he'd been banished
to some deep part of the abyss,
he'd be working his way back very
quickly. War was coming. We had
so much work to do."

—SADIE